SPACE, TIME, AND CONSCIOUSNESS

Omar Lopez, Ph.D.

SPACE, TIME, AND CONSCIOUSNESS

Cover Design by

www.srwalkerdesigns.com

FICTION4ALL

ACKNOWLEDGMENTS

I would like to express my deepest gratitude to the following individuals and organizations for their invaluable contributions to the creation of this book:

- Dr. Norman W. Wilson, for his insightful guidance, constructive comments, and thoughtful suggestions throughout the writing process.
- Stephen R. Walker of S.R. Walker Designs, for his exceptional design and meticulous editing of the book cover.
- Stuart Holland of Fiction4All, for his steadfast support and assistance in publishing my books.

Terms and Conditions

LEGAL NOTICE

PREFACE

When reading this book, it is essential to approach it with an open mind, as my intention is to demystify a complex subject and make it more accessible. Rather than crafting a lengthy 500-page book on the subject, I aimed to condense the intricate concepts of Space, Time, and Consciousness into a concise, easy-to-read format. My goal is to simplify these profound ideas, presenting them in a way that is both engaging and comprehensible, ensuring that readers of all backgrounds can grasp and appreciate the material without feeling overwhelmed.

Space and time are the framework within which the mind is constrained to construct its experience of reality.

— Immanuel Kant

Chapter 1: Introduction to Biocentrism

In a universe vast and mysterious, the quest to understand the nature of reality has driven human inquiry for millennia. One of the most revolutionary ideas in this quest is Biocentrism, a concept proposed by Dr. Robert Lanza. This theory suggests that life and consciousness are fundamental to the universe, rather than being mere byproducts of physical processes. In this chapter, we will explore the principles of Biocentrism, its implications, and how it challenges traditional views of reality.

The Essence of Biocentrism

Biocentrism, at its core, posits that life and biology are central to being, reality, and the cosmos. Dr. Lanza argues that the universe does not create life; instead, life creates the universe. This paradigm shift places biological processes at the heart of understanding the universe, suggesting that space, time, and the properties of matter are constructs of the conscious mind.

Key Principles of Biocentrism

1. **Reality is a Process That Involves Our Consciousness**: According to Biocentrism, what we perceive as reality is a process that requires consciousness. Without a conscious observer,

the universe would not exist in the same way. This principle challenges the traditional objective view of the universe existing independently of observation.

2. **The Universe is Fine-Tuned for Life**: Biocentrism suggests that the universe's fundamental constants and laws appear to be finely tuned to allow for the existence of life. This fine-tuning implies that life is not a random occurrence but a fundamental aspect of the universe.

3. **Space and Time are Constructs of the Mind**: Lanza proposes that space and time are not external realities but are ways in which our mind orders information. This idea aligns with findings in quantum mechanics, where the act of observation affects the state of a system.

4. **The Role of the Observer**: In Biocentrism, the observer plays a crucial role in shaping reality. The famous double-slit experiment in quantum physics illustrates how particles behave differently when observed, supporting the notion that the act of observation is fundamental to the behavior of particles.

Challenging Conventional Physics

Biocentrism stands in stark contrast to the traditional materialistic worldview, which holds that the universe is primarily composed of matter and that consciousness arises from complex interactions of matter. Instead, Biocentrism suggests that matter and energy are secondary phenomena arising from consciousness.

Implications for Physics and Cosmology

1. **Quantum Mechanics**: Biocentrism aligns with quantum mechanics, particularly the observer effect, where the mere act of observation can alter the state of particles. This suggests that consciousness plays a crucial role in the fundamental workings of the universe.

2. **Anthropic Principle**: The anthropic principle states that the universe must be compatible with conscious beings observing it. Biocentrism takes this a step further by suggesting that the universe is not just compatible with life but is actively shaped by it.

3. **Reconceptualizing Space and Time**: If space and time are constructs of the mind, then our understanding of the universe's expansion, the nature of black holes, and the Big Bang itself could be fundamentally altered. This perspec-

tive opens new avenues for theoretical physics and cosmology.

Philosophical and Ethical Implications

Beyond its scientific implications, Biocentrism also carries profound philosophical and ethical considerations. If life and consciousness are central to the universe, then the value of life takes on a new dimension. This view can influence how we approach issues such as environmental conservation, bioethics, and the search for extraterrestrial life.

A New Perspective on Life and Death

Biocentrism suggests that life and consciousness are continuous and fundamental aspects of reality. This perspective can alter our understanding of life and death, proposing that consciousness transcends the physical body. Such a view resonates with many spiritual and philosophical traditions, offering a bridge between science and spirituality.

Environmental Ethics

If life is central to the existence of the universe, then preserving and nurturing life becomes a primary ethical concern. Biocentrism encourages a holistic view of the environment, advocating for sustainable living and respect for all forms of life.

Criticisms and Controversies

As with any groundbreaking theory, Biocentrism has its critics. Some argue that it lacks empirical evidence and that its principles are more philosophical than scientific. Others contend that it does not provide testable predictions, a key criterion for scientific theories. However, proponents argue that Biocentrism offers a necessary paradigm shift that integrates consciousness into our understanding of the universe, addressing gaps in the current materialistic framework.

Biocentrism offers a revolutionary perspective on the nature of reality, placing life and consciousness at the center of the universe. By challenging conventional views and integrating findings from quantum mechanics, it opens new pathways for scientific inquiry and philosophical reflection. As we continue to explore the cosmos, Biocentrism reminds us that the observer and the observed are inextricably linked and that life itself may be the key to unlocking the mysteries of the universe.

"No phenomenon is a real phenomenon until it is an observed phenomenon."

— Robert Lanza

Chapter 2: The Foundations of Consciousness

Consciousness is one of the most profound and enigmatic phenomena in the universe. Despite centuries of philosophical inquiry and decades of scientific research, the nature of consciousness remains a topic of intense debate and investigation. This chapter aims to explore the foundational aspects of consciousness, delving into its definitions, historical context, key theories, and the challenges associated with understanding this complex subject.

Defining Consciousness

At its core, consciousness refers to the state of being aware of and able to think about one's own existence, sensations, thoughts, and surroundings. It encompasses a range of experiences from basic sensory perception to complex cognitive processes such as self-reflection and abstract thinking. However, consciousness is notoriously difficult to define comprehensively due to its subjective nature and the diversity of conscious experiences.

Several definitions have been proposed:

- **Phenomenal consciousness**: This refers to the subjective, qualitative aspects of experience, often described as "what it is like" to be in a particular state.

- **Access consciousness**: This involves the ability to report on mental states, use information in reasoning, and guide behavior.

- **Self-consciousness**: This is the awareness of oneself as an individual, separate from the environment and others.

Historical Context

The study of consciousness has ancient roots, with early philosophical inquiries found in the works of Greek philosophers such as Plato and Aristotle. Plato's allegory of the cave, for example, can be interpreted as a metaphor for the journey from ignorance to enlightenment, akin to the development of conscious awareness.

In the modern era, René Descartes' famous declaration "Cogito, ergo sum" ("I think, therefore I am") placed consciousness at the center of his philosophical system. Descartes posited that the mind and body are distinct entities (dualism), with consciousness being a fundamental attribute of the mind.

The 19th and 20th centuries saw significant advancements in the scientific study of consciousness, particularly with the development of psychology and neuroscience. William James, often regarded as the father of American psychology, described consciousness as a continuous stream, emphasizing its fluid and dynamic nature.

Key Theories of Consciousness

Numerous theories have been proposed to explain the nature and mechanisms of consciousness. Some of the most influential include:

- **Dualism**: As mentioned earlier, dualism, particularly Cartesian dualism, posits that the mind and body are separate substances. While this view has been largely superseded by more scientific approaches, it remains a pivotal historical perspective.

- **Materialism**: Materialist theories assert that consciousness arises from physical processes within the brain. The brain's complex neural networks and their interactions are thought to generate conscious experience. Prominent materialist theories include:

- **Integrated Information Theory (IIT)**: Proposed by Giulio Tononi, IIT posits that consciousness corresponds to the ability of a system to integrate information. The theory provides a mathematical framework for quantifying consciousness, suggesting that systems with high levels of integrated information (denoted as phi, Φ) possess greater consciousness.

- **Global Workspace Theory (GWT)**: Developed by Bernard Baars, GWT suggests that consciousness arises from the broadcasting of information within a "global workspace" in the brain. This workspace integrates information from various unconscious processes, making it accessible to different cognitive systems.

- **Panpsychism**: Panpsychism is a philosophical view that posits that consciousness is a fundamental and ubiquitous aspect of reality. According to this view, all matter possesses some degree of consciousness, albeit at varying levels of complexity.

Challenges in Understanding Consciousness

Despite significant progress, several challenges persist in the study of consciousness:

- **The Hard Problem**: Coined by philosopher David Chalmers, the "hard problem" of consciousness refers to the difficulty of explaining how and why subjective experiences arise from physical processes. While neuroscience can map neural correlates of consciousness, the transition from neural activity to conscious experience remains elusive.

- **Subjectivity**: Conscious experiences are inherently subjective and private, making them difficult to study using objective scientific methods. This subjectivity complicates the development of a comprehensive theory of consciousness.

- **Measurement**: Measuring consciousness, particularly in non-human animals and individuals with impaired communication, presents significant challenges. Developing reliable and valid metrics for assessing consciousness is an ongoing area of research.

- **Interdisciplinary Integration**: Consciousness research spans multiple disciplines, including philosophy, psychology, neuroscience, and computer science. Integrating insights from these diverse fields into a cohesive understanding is a complex and ongoing endeavor.

The foundation of consciousness is a rich and multifaceted topic, encompassing philosophical inquiry, scientific investigation, and profound questions about the nature of reality and self. While significant strides have been made in understanding consciousness, many mysteries remain. Continued interdisciplinary research, coupled with innovative theoretical and empirical approaches, holds promise for unraveling the enigma of consciousness and deepening our understanding of this fundamental aspect of human experience.

"The world you perceive is made of consciousness;
what you call matter is consciousness itself."

— Sri Nisargadatta Maharaj

Chapter 3: The Illusion of Space and Time

Throughout human history, space and time have been fundamental to our understanding of the universe. We measure distances in miles and kilometers, track events with clocks and calendars, and navigate our lives through the matrix of spatial and temporal coordinates. However, a growing body of philosophical and scientific thought suggests that space and time may not be the absolute realities we perceive them to be. Instead, they might be constructs of the human mind, tools for organizing our sensory experiences and making sense of the world around us.

The Philosophical Roots

The idea that space and time are illusions has deep philosophical roots. Ancient philosophers like Plato and later thinkers like Immanuel Kant laid the groundwork for this perspective. Plato's Allegory of the Cave suggested that the reality we perceive is but a shadow of the true forms that exist beyond our sensory experiences. Kant took this further, proposing that space and time are part of the innate structure of the human mind. According to Kant, they are a priori intuitions—fundamental frameworks that our minds impose on the raw data of experience.

The Relativity of Space and Time

In the early 20th century, Albert Einstein revolutionized our understanding of space and time with his theories of relativity. Special relativity introduced the concept that time and space are not fixed, but relative to the observer's state of motion. The faster you move, the more time dilates and distances contract—a phenomenon confirmed by numerous experiments.

General relativity further intertwined space and time into a single continuum: spacetime. This theory showed that massive objects like stars and planets distort spacetime, causing what we perceive as gravity. These insights challenged the Newtonian notion of absolute space and time, suggesting instead that our experience of these dimensions depends on our relative position and velocity.

Quantum Mechanics and Non-Locality

While relativity reshaped our macroscopic understanding of space and time, quantum mechanics did the same at the microscopic level. One of the most baffling aspects of quantum theory is entanglement, where particles become interconnected in such a way that the state of one instantly influences the state of another, regardless of distance. This phenomenon, famously derided by Einstein as "spooky action at a distance," suggests that the separation we perceive in space is illusory.

Moreover, experiments in quantum mechanics have demonstrated that the act of observation can affect the outcome of events. The double-slit experiment, for instance, shows that particles like electrons behave differently when observed, implying that the linear progression of time and the spatial separation between objects are not as objective as they seem.

The Mind as a Constructing Agent

If space and time are not fundamental aspects of the universe but constructs of the mind, it raises profound questions about the nature of reality. Cognitive science and neurobiology offer insights into how the brain creates these constructs. Our sensory organs receive raw data from the environment—light waves, sound waves, tactile stimuli—and the brain processes this information, constructing a coherent experience of space and time.

Neuroscientific research suggests that specific regions of the brain are involved in processing spatial and temporal information. The hippocampus, for instance, plays a crucial role in spatial navigation and memory formation, while the prefrontal cortex is involved in temporal organization and future planning. These brain activities demonstrate how space and time might be emergent properties of neural processes rather than external realities.

Cultural and Psychological Perspectives

Different cultures and individuals experience space and time differently, further supporting the idea that they are not absolute. Indigenous cultures often have conceptions of time that are cyclical rather than linear, and spatial understanding can vary significantly depending on language and environment. Psychologically, our perception of time can change with emotional states; moments of fear can stretch into eternity, while joyous occasions seem to pass in an instant.

The illusion of space and time challenges our deepest assumptions about the nature of reality. Philosophical traditions, scientific theories, and psychological insights converge on the idea that what we perceive as space and time may be constructs of our minds—useful fictions that help us navigate the complexity of existence. By understanding this, we open the door to new ways of thinking about the universe and our place within it, transcending the boundaries that once seemed insurmountable.

In the end, the journey through the illusion of space and time is a journey into the nature of consciousness itself, inviting us to explore the true essence of reality beyond the confines of our sensory experiences. As we continue to expand our understanding, we may discover that the universe is far more interconnected and profound than our traditional notions of space and time have allowed us o imagine.

"I have realized that the past and future are real illusions, that they exist in the present, which is what there is and all there is."

— Alan Watts

Chapter 4: Consciousness and Quantum Mechanics

Consciousness, the state of being aware of and able to think and perceive, is one of the most profound mysteries in science and philosophy. It encompasses everything from the sensory experiences and emotions we feel to the self-awareness and cognitive processing that enable us to reflect on our existence. Despite significant advances in neuroscience and psychology, the precise nature of consciousness remains elusive.

Classical Theories of Consciousness

Traditional approaches to understanding consciousness often rely on classical physics and biology. Neuroscientists typically view the brain as a complex network of neurons, where consciousness emerges from the interactions of billions of neurons and synaptic connections. Theories such as the Global Workspace Theory and Integrated Information Theory propose frameworks for how conscious experiences arise from these neural activities.

The Quantum Perspective

Quantum mechanics, the branch of physics that deals with the behavior of particles on the smallest scales, introduces a new dimension to the discussion of consciousness. Quantum mechanics is characterized by principles that differ dramatically from classical physics, including superposition, entanglement, and wave-particle duality. Some researchers propose that these quantum phenomena could play a crucial role in the workings of the mind.

Quantum Superposition and Consciousness

Superposition, the principle that a particle can exist in multiple states simultaneously until measured, is one of the most famous aspects of quantum mechanics. Some theories suggest that consciousness might arise from quantum superpositions within the brain's neural networks. For instance, the idea that neurons could be in superposition, where they are both firing and not firing simultaneously, could explain the fluid and dynamic nature of conscious experience.

Quantum Entanglement and Non-Locality

Quantum entanglement describes a situation where particles become interconnected in such a way that the state of one particle instantly influences the state of another, regardless of distance. This phenomenon, which Einstein famously referred to as "spooky action at a distance," has led some theorists to speculate that consciousness might involve non-local processes. If neurons or brain regions were entangled, it could mean that parts of the brain communicate instantaneously, providing a potential explanation for the unity of conscious experience.

The Orch-OR Theory

One of the most well-known and controversial quantum theories of consciousness is the Orchestrated Objective Reduction (Orch-OR) theory proposed by physicist Roger Penrose and anesthesiologist Stuart Hameroff. According to Orch-OR, consciousness arises from quantum computations in microtubules, which are structural components of neurons. They argue that these microtubules are capable of sustaining quantum superpositions, and that the collapse of these superpositions leads to moments of conscious awareness.

Challenges and Criticisms

While the integration of quantum mechanics into theories of consciousness is intriguing, it faces several challenges and criticisms. One major challenge is the issue of decoherence, which describes how quantum systems lose their quantum properties when interacting with the environment. The warm, wet, and noisy environment of the brain is typically seen as inhospitable to maintaining coherent quantum states. Critics argue that any potential quantum effects would decohere too quickly to influence neural processes.

Moreover, the leap from quantum phenomena to conscious experience is vast and not well understood. Many neuroscientists and philosophers remain skeptical of quantum consciousness theories, favoring explanations rooted in classical physics and neurobiology. They argue that the brain's complexity and the emergent properties of its networked structure are sufficient to explain consciousness without invoking quantum mechanics.

Bridging Quantum Mechanics and Consciousness

Despite these challenges, the idea that quantum mechanics could play a role in consciousness remains a tantalizing possibility. Some interdisciplinary researchers are exploring ways to bridge the gap between quantum physics and neuroscience. Advances in quantum biology, a field that investigates quantum effects in biological systems, offer some support for the feasibility of quantum processes in the brain.

Experiments in this domain are ongoing, seeking evidence of quantum coherence in neural structures or exploring how quantum algorithms might model cognitive processes.

The intersection of consciousness and quantum mechanics is a frontier of scientific inquiry that pushes the boundaries of our understanding. While current evidence does not definitively support the role of quantum mechanics in consciousness, the possibility remains an open and intriguing question. As research progresses, we may uncover new insights that either solidify or refute the quantum consciousness connection, ultimately bringing

us closer to unraveling the enigma of conscious experience.

**"Everything we call real is made of things that
cannot be regarded as real."**

— Niels Bohr

Chapter 5: The Observer Effect

The observer effect is a phenomenon that suggests the mere observation of a situation or phenomenon can influence the outcome. While the concept is widely discussed in various fields such as physics, psychology, and even social sciences, its implications and underlying mechanisms can vary significantly across different contexts. This chapter delves into the multifaceted nature of the observer effect, exploring its theoretical underpinnings, practical implications, and real-world examples.

The Observer Effect in Physics

In physics, the observer effect is often discussed in the context of quantum mechanics. At the quantum level, particles such as electrons can exist in multiple states or positions simultaneously, a phenomenon known as superposition. However, when an observer attempts to measure or observe these particles, the act of measurement collapses the superposition into a single state. This is most famously illustrated by the thought experiment known as Schrödinger's cat.

Schrödinger's Cat

In this thought experiment, a cat is placed in a sealed box with a radioactive atom, a Geiger counter, a vial of poison, and a hammer. If the Geiger counter detects radiation, the hammer breaks the vial, releasing the poison and killing the cat. According to quantum mechanics, until the box is opened and an observation is made, the cat is simultaneously alive and dead. The act of observation collapses this superposition into one of the two possible states: alive or dead.

Heisenberg's Uncertainty Principle

Another important concept related to the observer effect in physics is Heisenberg's Uncertainty Principle. This principle states that it is impossible to measure both the position and momentum of a particle with perfect accuracy. The more precisely one property is measured, the less precisely the other can be known. This inherent limitation is a direct consequence of the observer effect, as the act of measuring one property necessarily disturbs the other.

The Observer Effect in Psychology

In psychology, the observer effect is often referred to as the Hawthorne effect. This phenomenon was first observed during a series of studies at the Hawthorne Works factory in the 1920s and 1930s, where researchers found that workers' productivity increased when they knew they were being observed. The term has since been used to describe how individuals modify their behavior in response to being watched.

Social Facilitation

A related concept in psychology is social facilitation, which refers to the tendency for people to perform better on simple tasks and worse on complex tasks when in the presence of others. This is because the presence of an audience increases arousal, which can enhance performance on tasks that are well-practiced or straightforward but can impair performance on tasks that require significant cognitive effort or skill.

Self-Fulfilling Prophecies

The observer effect in psychology also intersects with the concept of self-fulfilling prophecies. This occurs when an individual's expectations about another person or situation influence their behavior in a way that causes the expectations to come true. For example, if a teacher believes that a student is particularly gifted, they may provide more encouragement and support, leading the student to perform better and thus confirming the teacher's original belief.

The Observer Effect in Social Sciences

In the social sciences, the observer effect is often considered in the context of research and data collection. When individuals know they are being studied, they may alter their behavior, consciously or unconsciously, to present themselves in a more favorable light. This can lead to skewed data and inaccurate conclusions.

Ethical Considerations

Researchers must navigate ethical considerations when designing studies to minimize the observer effect. In some cases, covert observation or deception may be used, but these methods raise their own ethical issues.

Informed consent and debriefing are crucial to ensure that participants are treated fairly and that the integrity of the research is maintained.

Case Studies and Examples

One well-known example of the observer effect in social sciences is the Stanford prison experiment. In this study, participants were assigned roles as either guards or prisoners in a simulated prison environment. The behavior of the participants changed dramatically as they embraced their roles, highlighting how the awareness of being part of a study can influence actions and attitudes.

Mitigating the Observer Effect

While it may be impossible to eliminate the observer effect entirely, researchers in various fields have developed strategies to minimize its impact. In physics, techniques such as indirect measurement and the use of control groups help mitigate the observer effect. In psychology and social sciences, methods such as double-blind studies, where neither the participants nor the researchers know who is receiving a particular treatment, can reduce bias.

Technological Solutions

Advancements in technology also offer new ways to address the observer effect. For example, unobtrusive monitoring tools and data collection methods can reduce the likelihood that participants alter their behavior due to awareness of being observed. Additionally, virtual reality and simulations provide opportunities to study behavior in controlled yet realistic environments.

The observer effect underscores the complex interplay between observation and reality. Whether in the realm of quantum particles or human behavior, the act of observing can alter the very phenomena being studied. Understanding and accounting for the observer effect is crucial for scientists, researchers, and practitioners across disciplines to draw accurate and meaningful conclusions from their observations and experiments. As our tools and techniques continue to evolve, so too will our ability to navigate and mitigate the observer effect, enhancing the reliability and validity of our findings.

"Every man's world picture is and always remains a construct of his mind and cannot be proved to have any other existence."

— Erwin Schrodinger

Chapter 6: The Multiverse and Consciousness

The concept of the multiverse has long fascinated scientists, philosophers, and writers. At its core, the multiverse suggests the existence of multiple, perhaps infinite, universes parallel to our own. Each universe within the multiverse could have different physical laws, constants, and even different versions of ourselves. But how does this idea intersect with the nature of consciousness? This chapter explores the intriguing relationship between the multiverse and consciousness, delving into theoretical physics, philosophy, and the implications for our understanding of reality.

The Multiverse Theory

The multiverse theory arises from various interpretations of quantum mechanics and cosmology. Among the prominent multiverse hypotheses are:

1. **The Many-Worlds Interpretation**: Proposed by Hugh Everett III in 1957, this interpretation of quantum mechanics suggests that all possible outcomes of quantum measurements are realized in some "world" or universe. Thus, every decision or random event spawns a new universe.

2. **Bubble Universes (Eternal Inflation)**: According to this theory, proposed by physicist Alan Guth and others, our universe is one of many bubbles that formed during a rapid expansion after the Big Bang. Each bubble universe could have different physical properties.

3. **The Brane Multiverse**: Stemming from string theory, this hypothesis posits that our universe is a 3-dimensional brane embedded in a higher-dimensional space, with other branes existing parallel to ours.

4. **The Quantum Multiverse**: In this view, each quantum event results in a branching of the universe into a multitude of new universes, each representing a different possible outcome.

These theories, while varied, share the idea that our reality is just one of many, potentially limitless, realities.

Consciousness: A Complex Enigma

Consciousness remains one of the greatest mysteries of science and philosophy. It encompasses our awareness, thoughts, feelings, and perceptions. Despite extensive study, the fundamental nature of consciousness—how it arises from the brain's physical processes—remains elusive. Several key questions include:

- **What is the relationship between mind and matter?**
- **Can consciousness exist independently of the physical body?**
- **How does consciousness emerge from neural activity?**

Various theories attempt to explain consciousness, from physicalist perspectives that see it as an emergent property of brain processes to dualist views that regard mind and matter as distinct.

Intersections of the Multiverse and Consciousness

1. **Quantum Consciousness**: Some theorists, such as Roger Penrose and Stuart Hameroff, propose that consciousness is linked to quantum processes within the brain. If true, this raises the possibility that consciousness might be connected to the quantum multiverse. Each decision and observation could not only shape our reality but also influence and interact with parallel universes.

2. **Transpersonal Experiences**: Mystical experiences, near-death experiences, and certain altered states of consciousness often describe realities beyond our known universe. These subjective experiences may hint at consciousness's ability to transcend physical boundaries, suggesting a connection to the broader multiverse.

3. **Consciousness as a Universal Constant**:
   Some philosophers argue that consciousness
   might be a fundamental aspect of the universe,
   much like space-time or matter. This
   panpsychist view posits that consciousness is a
   universal feature present to some degree in all
   things, potentially varying across different
   universes in the multiverse.

Implications for Understanding Reality

The interplay between the multiverse and consciousness
challenges our conventional understanding of reality in
several profound ways:

1. **Free Will and Determinism**: If every possible
   choice we make spawns a new universe, what
   does this mean for free will? Are we merely
   following predetermined paths across different
   universes, or do our choices actively create
   new realities?

2. **The Nature of Self**: In a multiverse, there
   could be countless versions of ourselves. What
   defines our "true" self if our consciousness
   could potentially experience different realities?
   This raises questions about identity, continuity,
   and the essence of what it means to be "you."

3. **Life and Death**: The concept of the multiverse might offer new perspectives on life and death. If consciousness can transcend individual universes, what happens to our consciousness after death? Could it shift to another universe or exist in a different form?

4. **Ethics and Responsibility**: Understanding our place in a multiverse could have ethical implications. If our actions can create or influence other universes, what responsibility do we have for those other realities?

The relationship between the multiverse and consciousness is a frontier of thought that blurs the lines between science and philosophy. While we have only begun to scratch the surface of these profound questions, the potential insights they offer could revolutionize our understanding of reality, our place within it, and the nature of our own minds. As we continue to explore these ideas, we may find that the boundaries of what we know are as limitless as the multiverse itself.

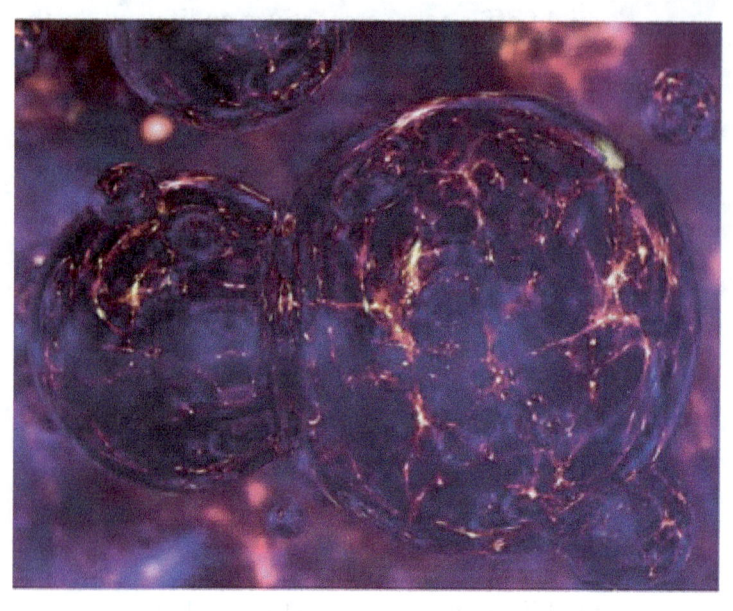

"I believe we exist in a multiverse of universes."

— Michio Kaku

Chapter 7: Consciousness and Evolution

Consciousness, the essence of our subjective experiences, has intrigued philosophers, scientists, and thinkers for centuries. It is the self-aware, introspective quality of the mind that allows us to experience the world, ponder our existence, and engage in complex thought processes. Understanding consciousness necessitates an exploration of its evolutionary origins, a journey that interweaves the threads of biology, psychology, and neurology. This chapter delves into the evolutionary development of consciousness, exploring its roots, adaptive significance, and the ongoing quest to unravel its mysteries.

The Evolutionary Roots of Consciousness

The story of consciousness begins with the earliest forms of life on Earth. Primitive organisms, such as single-celled bacteria, exhibit basic responsiveness to their environments. This reactivity is a fundamental precursor to consciousness, allowing organisms to adapt and survive. As life evolved, so did the complexity of these responses.

The emergence of the nervous system marked a significant milestone in the evolution of consciousness. Early multicellular organisms developed simple neural networks, enabling more sophisticated interactions with their surroundings. These neural networks evolved into centralized nervous systems, culminating in the development of brains in more complex organisms.

The Adaptive Value of Consciousness

Consciousness provides several adaptive advantages that have driven its evolution. One primary advantage is the ability to integrate sensory information to make informed decisions. In early animal life, the capacity to perceive threats and opportunities allowed for more effective survival strategies. The evolution of sensory organs and the central nervous system facilitated the processing of this information, enhancing an organism's ability to respond to environmental changes.

Another significant advantage is the role of consciousness in social interactions. As animals began to live in more complex social structures, the ability to understand and predict the behavior of others became crucial. Empathy, theory of mind, and social learning are all facets of consciousness that have evolved to support social cohesion and cooperation. In human societies, these abilities underpin complex social dynamics and cultural evolution.

Consciousness in Non-Human Animals

The study of consciousness in non-human animals provides valuable insights into its evolutionary development. Various species exhibit behaviors suggestive of consciousness, such as problem-solving, self-recognition, and emotional responses. For example, primates, dolphins, and elephants demonstrate high levels of self-awareness and cognitive complexity, indicating a degree of conscious experience.

Research on animal consciousness often focuses on the presence of subjective experiences and the capacity for metacognition – the ability to think about one's own thoughts. Studies on mirror self-recognition, for instance, reveal that some animals can recognize themselves in a mirror, suggesting a level of self-awareness previously thought to be uniquely human.

The Human Consciousness

Human consciousness represents the pinnacle of evolutionary complexity. Our cognitive abilities, emotional depth, and capacity for abstract thought are unparalleled in the animal kingdom. Language, culture, and art are expressions of our advanced consciousness, enabling us to communicate complex ideas, share knowledge across generations, and create rich, symbolic worlds.

The human brain, with its intricate networks of neurons, is the epicenter of our conscious experience. The prefrontal cortex, in particular, is associated with higher-order functions such as planning, decision-making, and self-reflection. The intricate interplay between different brain regions facilitates the emergence of consciousness, though the exact mechanisms remain a subject of intense research and debate.

Challenges and Theories in Understanding Consciousness

Despite significant advancements, the nature of consciousness continues to elude complete understanding. Several theories attempt to explain how consciousness arises from neural processes. One prominent theory is the Global Workspace Theory, which posits that consciousness arises from the integration of information in a central "workspace" within the brain, accessible to different cognitive processes.

Another influential perspective is the Integrated Information Theory (IIT), which suggests that consciousness corresponds to the integration of information across the brain's neural networks. According to IIT, the degree of consciousness is determined by the level of informational integration, with more complex integrations resulting in richer conscious experiences.

The evolution of consciousness is a testament to the incredible complexity and adaptability of life on Earth. From the rudimentary responses of single-celled organisms to the profound self-awareness of humans, consciousness has evolved as a multifaceted phenomenon with deep biological roots. While much remains to be discovered, the study of consciousness continues to illuminate the intricate relationship between the brain, mind, and the natural world, offering profound insights into the very nature of existence.

"There is no life without consciousness; there is no consciousness without life."

— Annie Besant

Chapter 8: Consciousness and the Mind-Body Connection

Consciousness and the mind-body connection are two of the most profound and intriguing subjects in the study of human nature. For centuries, philosophers, scientists, and theologians have pondered the nature of consciousness and its relationship to the physical body. In this chapter, we will explore the complexities of consciousness, the theories that attempt to explain it, and the intricate ways in which the mind and body are interconnected.

The Nature of Consciousness

Consciousness is often described as the state of being aware of and able to think about oneself and the environment. It encompasses a wide range of experiences, from the sensory perceptions of the external world to the inner experiences of thoughts, emotions, and self-awareness.

Levels of Consciousness

1. **Basic Awareness:** This involves the sensory experiences that make us aware of our surroundings. It includes the perception of colors, sounds, textures, and other sensory inputs.
2. **Self-Awareness:** This is the recognition of oneself as an individual separate from the environment and other individuals. It includes the

ability to reflect on one's thoughts, feelings, and experiences.

3. **Meta-Consciousness:** This is the awareness of one's own consciousness. It involves higher-order thinking about one's mental states and processes.

Theories of Consciousness

Dualism

Dualism is the theory that the mind and body are fundamentally different substances. This view, famously advocated by René Descartes, posits that the mind is a non-physical entity that interacts with the physical body. Descartes argued that while the body operates according to physical laws, the mind is capable of thought and reasoning, which cannot be explained solely by physical processes.

Materialism

Materialism asserts that everything about consciousness can be explained in terms of physical processes in the brain. According to this view, mental states are brain states, and consciousness arises from the interactions of neurons and biochemical processes. This theory is supported by advances in neuroscience that have identified specific brain regions and networks associated with different aspects of consciousness.

Functionalism

Functionalism suggests that mental states are defined by their functional roles rather than by their physical makeup. According to functionalists, what matters is not what the mind is made of, but what it does. This perspective allows for the possibility that artificial intelligence or other non-biological systems could possess consciousness if they perform the same functions as human minds.

Integrated Information Theory (IIT)

IIT proposes that consciousness arises from the integration of information within a system. The theory suggests that a system is conscious to the extent that it has a high degree of informational integration. This means that a conscious system cannot be decomposed into independent parts without losing the essence of its conscious experience.

The Mind-Body Connection

The mind-body connection refers to the complex interactions between the mental processes and the physical state of the body. This relationship is evident in various phenomena, such as the placebo effect, psychosomatic illnesses, and the impact of mental states on physical health.

Psychoneuroimmunology

Psychoneuroimmunology is the study of how psychological factors, the nervous system, and the immune system interact. Research in this field has shown that stress and emotional states can significantly influence immune function. For instance, chronic stress can suppress immune responses, making individuals more susceptible to illnesses.

The Placebo Effect

The placebo effect demonstrates the power of the mind in influencing physical health. When patients believe they are receiving treatment, they often experience real improvements in their condition, even if the treatment has no therapeutic value. This phenomenon underscores the importance of psychological factors in the healing process.

Mindfulness and Meditation

Mindfulness and meditation practices have been shown to have profound effects on both mental and physical health. These practices enhance self-awareness and emotional regulation while also reducing stress, improving immune function, and lowering blood pressure. The benefits of mindfulness highlight the bidirectional relationship between the mind and body.

Consciousness and Personal Identity

Consciousness is central to our sense of personal identity. Our continuous stream of thoughts, memories, and experiences creates a coherent narrative of who we are. However, this sense of self is not static; it evolves over time with new experiences and changing perspectives.

Memory and Identity

Memory plays a crucial role in maintaining personal identity. Our memories connect our past selves to our present, allowing us to perceive ourselves as the same person over time. Disorders that affect memory, such as amnesia, can profoundly disrupt one's sense of identity.

The Narrative Self

The narrative self refers to the ongoing story we tell about ourselves. It is constructed from our memories, beliefs, goals, and values. This narrative is not always accurate or complete, but it provides a framework for understanding our place in the world and our relationships with others.

The study of consciousness and the mind-body connection touches on some of the most fundamental questions about human existence. While much remains to be understood, ongoing research continues to unravel the complexities of how our minds work and how they are intertwined with our physical bodies. As we deepen our understanding, we gain not only scientific insights but also a greater appreciation for the intricate nature of our own consciousness and its profound connection to our physical being.

"It is possible that I am dreaming right now and that all of my perceptions are false."

— Rene Descartes

Chapter 9: The Unity of Consciousness

The unity of consciousness has intrigued philosophers, psychologists, and neuroscientists for centuries. It refers to the coherent and integrated nature of our conscious experience, where all the different elements of our perception, thought, and sensation come together to form a single, unified experience. This chapter explores the philosophical underpinnings, psychological mechanisms, and neuroscientific findings related to the unity of consciousness.

Philosophical Perspectives

Philosophically, the unity of consciousness addresses how diverse sensory inputs and mental states converge into a singular conscious experience. Descartes, one of the early proponents of this idea, posited that the self is a single, indivisible entity. Kant further developed this notion, suggesting that unity is necessary for the possibility of experience and self-consciousness. According to Kant, the mind must synthesize sensory data into a coherent whole to perceive objects and events.

More contemporary philosophers, such as David Chalmers and Ned Block, have debated the nature of this unity. Chalmers, for instance, distinguishes between the easy problems of consciousness (which involve explaining cognitive functions) and the hard problem (which involves explaining subjective experience). The unity of consciousness falls into the hard problem category, as it seeks to understand how these unified experiences arise from the brain's complex activity.

Psychological Mechanisms

From a psychological perspective, the unity of consciousness involves several mechanisms that integrate sensory information and cognitive processes. Attention plays a crucial role in this integration, as it allows the mind to focus on relevant stimuli while filtering out the irrelevant. Selective attention ensures that disparate pieces of information are combined into a coherent experience.

The Gestalt principles of perception, such as proximity, similarity, and continuity, also contribute to this unity. These principles describe how our minds naturally group elements into whole forms, making sense of complex visual scenes. For instance, when we see a tree, we don't perceive individual leaves and branches independently but rather as parts of a single object.

Neuroscientific Insights

Neuroscience has provided significant insights into how the brain achieves the unity of consciousness. Research suggests that synchronized neural activity, particularly in the gamma frequency range, plays a vital role in binding different sensory inputs into a unified experience. This neural synchronization occurs across different brain regions, facilitating communication and integration of information.

One influential theory in this regard is the Global Workspace Theory (GWT), proposed by Bernard Baars. GWT posits that consciousness arises from the broadcasting of information to a "global workspace" in the brain, where different cognitive processes converge. This workspace allows for the integration of various sensory inputs and thoughts into a cohesive experience.

Additionally, the Default Mode Network (DMN), a network of brain regions that shows increased activity during rest and self-referential thought, has been implicated in maintaining the unity of consciousness. The DMN is thought to play a role in integrating past experiences with current perceptions, contributing to a unified sense of self and continuity over time.

Challenges and Controversies

Despite significant progress, the unity of consciousness remains a deeply contested and complex issue. One major challenge is understanding how the brain integrates information from different sensory modalities and cognitive processes, given the distributed nature of neural activity. Some researchers argue that the unity of consciousness may not be as seamless as it appears, pointing to phenomena like split-brain patients, where the severing of the corpus callosum leads to seemingly independent streams of consciousness within the same individual.

Moreover, the subjective nature of conscious experience poses a significant challenge to objective scientific inquiry. While we can measure neural correlates of consciousness, capturing the essence of what it feels like to have a unified conscious experience remains elusive.

The unity of consciousness is a multifaceted concept that sits at the intersection of philosophy, psychology, and neuroscience. It addresses one of the most profound questions about the human mind: how do our diverse perceptions, thoughts, and sensations coalesce into a single, coherent experience? While significant strides have been made in understanding the mechanisms underlying this unity, many questions remain unanswered.

As research continues to evolve, the unity of consciousness will undoubtedly remain a central topic in the quest to unravel the mysteries of the human mind.

"Things which we see are not by themselves what we see ... It remains completely unknown to us what the objects may be by themselves and apart from the receptivity of our senses. We know nothing but our manner of perceiving them."

— Immanuel Kant

Chapter 10: The Nature of Space and Time

Space-Time Unity

The interconnected nature of space and time in the fabric of reality is a fascinating concept that has captivated the minds of philosophers and scientists alike. In this chapter, we will delve into the concept of space-time unity and explore how it helps us understand the physical world.

Space-time unity refers to the idea that space and time are not separate entities, but rather interconnected aspects of a single fabric that encompasses the universe. This concept arose from our understanding of Einstein's theory of relativity, which revolutionized our understanding of the nature of space and time.

According to Einstein's theory, space and time are not absolute and unchanging, but rather dynamic and influenced by the presence of mass and energy. Space-time is like a flexible fabric that can be stretched and warped by the presence of massive objects. This warping of space-time is what gives rise to the force of gravity, which governs the motion of objects in the universe.

An important consequence of space-time unity is that the perception of time can be affected by the presence of massive objects or high speeds. This phenomenon, known as time dilation, means that time can flow at different rates for observers in different gravitational fields or moving at different speeds. This has been experimentally verified and has important implications for our understanding of the universe.

Space-time unity also helps to explain some of the mysteries of the universe, such as the cosmic expansion and the concept of black holes. The expanding universe, as observed through the redshift of distant galaxies, can be understood as the stretching of space-time itself. Black holes, on the other hand, represent regions of space-time that have been so severely warped by massive objects that nothing, not even light, can escape their gravitational pull.

By embracing the concept of space-time unity, we are able to connect the dots between space, time, and metaphysics. It allows us to view the universe as a cohesive system, where the laws of physics govern the behavior of matter and energy in the space-time fabric. This perspective opens up new avenues of exploration and understanding, pushing the boundaries of our knowledge.

Spacetime and Entropy

In the study of the universe, one fascinating area of exploration is the relationship between spacetime and entropy. Spacetime, as Einstein postulated, is a four-dimensional construct that encompasses three dimensions of space and one dimension of time. It provides the framework within which all physical events occur. On the other hand, entropy is a measure of the disorder or randomness in a system. It plays a crucial role in understanding the behavior and evolution of various phenomena.

A deep understanding of the relationship between spacetime and entropy allows us to explore the fundamental principles that govern the universe. It sheds light on the origins of complexity, the arrow of time, and the nature of black holes.

Entropy plays a fundamental role in shaping the evolution of spacetime. As the universe expands, entropy increases, leading to the growth of disorder and randomness. This increase in entropy influences the behavior of matter and energy, ultimately shaping the evolution of spacetime.

Furthermore, the relationship between entropy and spacetime can be observed in the formation and behavior of black holes. When matter collapses under the influence of gravity, it reaches a point of infinite density known as a singularity. At this point, the entropy of the matter becomes concentrated in an extremely small region of spacetime. This concentration of entropy is what gives rise to the immense gravitational pull of black holes.

Additionally, the study of entropy in the context of spacetime allows us to explore the concept of the arrow of time. Entropy tends to increase as time progresses, leading to the irreversibility of certain processes. Understanding how entropy influences the behavior of spacetime provides insights into why time appears to flow in a specific direction.

Beyond Space and Time

When we delve into the depths of abstract and speculative theories, we enter a realm beyond our conventional understanding of space and time. It is in this theoretical landscape that we encounter fascinating concepts that question the very fabric of our reality. In this chapter, we will explore the intriguing ideas that lie beyond space and time.

One of the theories that captivates the minds of physicists and cosmologists is string theory. This concept suggests that the fundamental building blocks of the universe are not point-like particles but tiny, vibrating strings. These strings vibrate at different frequencies, giving rise to various particles and forces. String theory allows for the existence of multiple dimensions beyond the three spatial dimensions and one temporal dimension that we are familiar with. These extra dimensions are compactified, meaning they are curled up and hidden from our everyday perception.

In the realm of multidimensional space, another concept that arises is branes. A brane, short for membrane, is a theoretical object that can exist in higher-dimensional space. These branes can take various forms, such as plane-like or curved structures. They can have different dimensions and are believed to be the source of certain physical phenomena, such as gravity. The interaction and dynamics of branes in multidimensional space open up new possibilities for understanding our universe.

Exploring dimensions beyond space and time not only challenges our preconceived notions but also raises profound questions about the nature of reality. How do these dimensions interact with our familiar three-dimensional world? What impact do they have on the fabric of space and time? These questions lie at the intersection of physics, metaphysics, and philosophy.

In conclusion, venturing into the realm of abstract and speculative theories about dimensions beyond space and time leads us to intriguing ideas such as string theory, branes, and multidimensional space.

With each step, we uncover deeper layers of our existence and challenge the boundaries of our understanding. Join us as we dive into the mysteries of the cosmos and explore the fascinating connections between space, time, and metaphysics.

"A human being is a part of the whole called by us
universe, a part limited in time and space. He
experiences himself, his thoughts and feeling as
something separated from the rest, a kind of optical
delusion of his consciousness. This delusion is a kind
of prison for us, restricting us to our personal desires
and to affection for a few persons nearest to us. Our
task must be to free ourselves from this prison by
widening our circle of compassion to embrace all
living creatures and the whole of nature in its
beauty."

— Albert Einstein

Chapter 11: Concepts of Infinity

Infinity in Space

Space, as we understand it, is a seemingly infinite expanse that stretches out in all directions. It is a concept that both fascinates and perplexes us. The sheer vastness of space is difficult for the human mind to comprehend. But what exactly does it mean for space to be infinite? And how does this concept of infinity relate to the boundlessness of the cosmos?

When we talk about space being infinite, we mean that it has no boundaries or edges. It goes on forever, without any limit. This is a mind-boggling idea, as it suggests that there is no end to the universe. It is like trying to imagine a number that goes on forever, without ever reaching a final value.

One way to understand this concept is by thinking about the expansion of the universe. The universe is constantly expanding, with galaxies moving farther apart from each other. This expansion has been going on for billions of years and shows no signs of stopping. If the universe were finite, eventually all the matter and energy within it would reach a point where it could expand no further. But because the universe is infinite, it can continue expanding indefinitely.

This concept of infinity also ties into the idea of parallel universes and alternate dimensions. Some theories propose that there are multiple universes existing alongside our own, each with its own laws of physics and dimensions. These alternate dimensions may have different spatial dimensions, beyond the three that we are familiar with. In this way, the concept of infinity extends beyond just the vastness of space, but also to the potential existence of infinite dimensions.

The idea of infinite spatial dimensions may seem difficult to grasp, but it is a concept that has fascinated scientists and philosophers for centuries. It challenges our intuitive understanding of the world and opens up new possibilities for how the universe might be structured.

In the realm of physics, theories such as String Theory and M-Theory propose the existence of more than just the three spatial dimensions we are familiar with. These theories suggest that there could be additional dimensions, perhaps curled up and hidden within the fabric of space-time. If this is true, it means that the universe might be far more complex than we can currently comprehend.

One way to visualize these additional dimensions is to think about a garden hose. In our three-dimensional world, a garden hose appears as a tube. But if you were to zoom in on a microscopic level, you would see that the hose is made up of tiny curled-up dimensions. These extra dimensions are too small for us to detect with our current technology, but they could have a profound impact on the fundamental laws of physics.

So why do scientists and philosophers explore the concept of infinite spatial dimensions? It is not just an intellectual exercise or a way to entertain abstract ideas. Understanding the nature of space and the potential existence of infinite dimensions could have practical implications for our understanding of the universe and the development of future technologies.

In summary, the concept of infinity in space is a fascinating topic that challenges our understanding of the vastness of the universe. It opens up new possibilities for the structure of the cosmos and the existence of additional dimensions. By delving into these ideas, we can gain a deeper understanding of the mysteries of space, time, and metaphysics.

Infinity in Time

Time, a concept that has deeply intrigued philosophers and scientists alike, is often contemplated in relation to infinity. As humans, we are bound by the passing of time, experiencing it as a linear progression from one moment to the next. However, when we delve into the depths of metaphysics and explore the concept of infinite time, a whole new realm of possibilities emerges.

When we consider infinity in the context of time, we are faced with thought-provoking questions. Does time have a beginning and an end, or does it stretch infinitely in both directions? Can time exist outside the boundaries of our universe, or is it intricately tied to the fabric of space? These questions challenge our understanding of reality and push us to explore the mysteries of the cosmos.

As we contemplate the concept of infinite time, both philosophical and scientific perspectives come into play. Philosophers have long pondered the nature of time, seeking to understand its fundamental essence. From Aristotle's belief in a cyclical view of time to Augustine's concept of time as a present-minded experience, various philosophical frameworks have been proposed throughout history.

On the other hand, scientific advancements have provided us with valuable insights into the nature of time. The theory of relativity, put forth by Albert Einstein, introduced the concept of spacetime, where time is interwoven with the three dimensions of space. This revolutionary theory allows us to comprehend the relativity of time, where its passage can differ depending on the observer's relative motion or gravitational field.

Within the realm of metaphysics, the idea of infinity in time expands our understanding of existence. It opens up possibilities of multiple universes, where time may flow in different directions or exhibit entirely different properties. Some theories postulate the existence of parallel universes or alternate timelines, where time branches off into infinite possibilities.

Furthermore, the concept of infinity in time challenges our perception of cause and effect. If time is infinite, does every event that has occurred or will occur already exist within the vast expanse of time? Or does time itself unfold and create new moments as it progresses endlessly? These metaphysical quandaries force us to confront the limitations of our human comprehension and envision a reality that transcends our temporal boundaries.

In conclusion, the notion of infinity in the context of time offers a captivating exploration into the mysteries of existence. Through both philosophical contemplation and scientific inquiry, we can push the boundaries of our understanding and delve deeper into the enigmatic nature of time. As we continue to unravel the complexities of the universe, the concept of infinite time will remain a profound subject of exploration for those interested in the interplay between space, time, and metaphysics.

Infinity in Mathematics

Infinity is a concept that has fascinated mathematicians, philosophers, and scientists alike. It plays a crucial role in various mathematical concepts and calculations, as well as in our understanding of space, time, and metaphysics. In this chapter, we will delve deeper into the concept of infinity in mathematics, exploring its different types and their properties.

Before we begin, it is important to note that infinity is not a number, but rather a concept that represents something endless or unbounded. In mathematics, infinity is often used to describe sets or processes that continue indefinitely.

One of the key aspects of infinity in mathematics is the understanding of different types of infinities. While infinity itself is infinite, there are different magnitudes or sizes of infinity. This may sound counterintuitive, but it is a fascinating concept that mathematicians have been able to explore and understand.

Cantor, a German mathematician, made significant contributions to the study of different infinities. He showed that not all infinities are the same size. For example, there are more real numbers between 0 and 1 than there are counting numbers (1, 2, 3, ...). This discovery opened up a whole new field of mathematics called set theory, which deals with the properties and relationships of sets.

Another interesting aspect of infinity is that it can be approached as a limit in calculus. In calculus, we often encounter situations where a value becomes arbitrarily large, approaching infinity. This concept is fundamental to understanding functions, rates of change, and the behavior of systems.

Infinity also has applications in geometry, where it can be used to describe points at an infinite distance. For example, in projective geometry, points at infinity play an essential role in maintaining the symmetry and completeness of geometric systems.

Furthermore, infinity has philosophical implications, as it challenges our understanding of space, time, and the nature of reality. Many philosophical debates and theories center around the concept of infinity and its implications for our understanding of the universe.

The concept of infinity is a fundamental and intriguing aspect of mathematics. Its presence in various mathematical concepts, calculations, and philosophical discussions underscores its significance in shaping our understanding of the world around us.

"The world is a drama, staged in a dream."

— Guru Nanak

Chapter 12: Temporal and Spatial Dimensions

Higher Dimensions in Physics

When it comes to understanding space, time, and metaphysics, many people are intrigued by the possibility of additional dimensions beyond the three that we experience in our everyday lives. This exploration of higher dimensions falls under the subfield of physics that has captivated the minds of scientists and philosophers alike.

One theory that attempts to explain the existence of additional spatial dimensions is the Kaluza-Klein theory. Developed in the early 20th century by Theodor Kaluza and Oskar Klein, this theory suggests that there may be extra dimensions that are too small to be observed directly. These additional dimensions, often referred to as compactified dimensions, are believed to be curled up and hidden from our perception. Kaluza-Klein theory aims to unify the forces of gravity and electromagnetism by introducing the concept of a higher-dimensional space.

Another intriguing idea is the concept of extra dimensions in string theory. According to this theory, all fundamental particles are not point-like objects but rather tiny strings vibrating in higher-dimensional space. These extra dimensions, often visualized as tiny curled-up spaces, play a crucial role in string theory's attempts to reconcile gravity with quantum mechanics. While string theory proposes the existence of multiple dimensions, it is currently still a subject of active research and debate within the scientific community.

Exploring the concept of higher dimensions in physics provides fascinating insights into the fundamental nature of our universe. It challenges our perceptions of space and time and opens up new possibilities for understanding the underlying principles that govern our reality.

Multidimensional Space-Time

The concept of multidimensional space-time fabric has intrigued scientists and philosophers alike for centuries. It is a concept that attempts to explain the interconnectedness of space, time, and the very fabric of reality itself. This chapter aims to delve into the intricacies of multidimensional space-time, providing a deeper understanding of how these dimensions may interact within the fabric of our universe. So, let us embark on this fascinating journey as we explore the world of multidimensional space-time.

Our exploration begins with a fundamental question: What exactly is multidimensional space-time? In essence, it is a theoretical framework that extends the traditional three dimensions of space (length, width, and height) to incorporate additional dimensions. These additional dimensions, often referred to as higher dimensions, go beyond our intuitive perception of reality and provide a rich tapestry upon which the universe unfolds.

One of the most famous theories that incorporate higher-dimensional structures in the fabric of reality is string theory. This theoretical framework suggests that the fundamental building blocks of the universe are not point-like particles but rather tiny, vibrating strings. These strings can exist in a space-time fabric that encompasses more than the three dimensions we experience in our daily lives. In fact, string theory requires the existence of at least nine spatial dimensions and one temporal dimension, resulting in a rich and complex multidimensional space-time fabric.

The notion of multidimensional space-time may seem perplexing at first, but it offers a powerful framework for understanding the fundamental nature of our universe. It allows for the possibility of hidden dimensions, curled up and compactified in ways that are beyond our current perception. These hidden dimensions may hold the key to unlocking the mysteries of dark matter and dark energy, which are believed to make up the majority of the universe's content. By embracing the concept of multidimensional space-time, we open ourselves to new possibilities and avenues of exploration in the vast realm of physics and metaphysics.

As we conclude this chapter, we invite you to contemplate the profound implications of multidimensional space-time. It challenges our traditional views of reality and invites us to question the very nature of our existence. By delving into the depths of this fascinating concept, we gain a deeper appreciation for the interconnectedness of space, time, and metaphysics. So, let us continue our exploration, venturing further into the mysteries that lie within the multidimensional space-time fabric.

Time Travel and Extra Dimensions

Time travel has long been a fascination of human beings, capturing our imaginations and sparking endless debate about the nature of space, time, and metaphysics. Combining this fascination with the possibility of extra dimensions opens up even greater possibilities and reveals the depths of our curiosity and understanding.

When we consider the concept of time travel, we inevitably come face to face with the question of whether it can be achieved through extra dimensions. Extra dimensions, beyond the familiar three spatial dimensions and the dimension of time, have been postulated by various theories in physics and mathematics. These additional dimensions, if they exist, may offer portals or pathways through which time travel could take place.

One of the intriguing ideas in physics is the concept of wormholes, which are hypothetical shortcuts connecting two distant points in spacetime. These wormholes could potentially be accessed through extra dimensions, allowing for the possibility of navigating through time and space in a non-linear fashion.

However, the feasibility of time travel through extra dimensions is highly speculative and fraught with paradoxes. The famous grandfather paradox, for instance, raises the question of what would happen if someone were to travel back in time and kill their own grandfather before their parent was born. Such paradoxes highlight the complexities and contradictions that arise when contemplating time travel.

The Philosophy of Space-Time

Plato's Theory of Forms is a philosophical concept that explores the nature of reality and its relationship with space, time, and metaphysics. This theory proposes that there is an ideal realm of existence, separate from the physical world, where perfect and unchanging Forms exist.

In this ideal realm, Forms represent the essences or perfect archetypes of all things that exist in the physical world. These Forms, such as beauty, justice, and truth, are timeless and unchanging. They are the ultimate reality, while the physical world we perceive is merely a flawed reflection or imitation of these Forms.

This theory has profound implications for our understanding of reality. It suggests that our perception of the physical world is limited and imperfect, as we can only experience imperfect manifestations of the perfect Forms. For example, when we encounter something, we consider beautiful in the physical world, it is merely an imperfect reflection of the Form of beauty.

Furthermore, the Theory of Forms challenges our understanding of space and time. In the ideal realm, Forms are not bound by the limitations of space and time. They exist independently of our physical world, which is subject to change and decay. This raises questions about the nature of existence and the relationship between the eternal Forms and the transient physical world.

Plato's Theory of Forms has been a subject of extensive philosophical debate and interpretation. It has influenced numerous thinkers and continues to spark discussions about the nature of reality, perception, and the metaphysical foundations of our existence.

Kant's Transcendental Aesthetic

Immanuel Kant's philosophical framework provides a deep understanding of space and time, and how they relate to our perception of reality. Kant's ideas, expressed in his work Critique of Pure Reason, have had a profound impact on metaphysics and our understanding of the world.

One key aspect of Kant's framework is the role of the transcendental aesthetic. This concept explores how our intuition of space and time shapes our experience of the world. The transcendental aesthetic is the foundation upon which our cognition operates, allowing us to organize and structure our sensory perceptions.

Kant argued that space and time are not external and independent entities but rather a priori forms of intuition that are inherent to our consciousness. In other words, space and time are not merely perceptions of external objects; they are the fundamental structures through which we perceive the world.

According to Kant, space is the form of outer intuition, while time is the form of inner intuition. Space provides the framework for organizing our perception of objects in relation to one another, while time allows us to experience events as temporal sequences.

Kant's transcendental aesthetic also introduces the concept of synthetic a priori judgments. These are judgments that go beyond our immediate sensory experience and require the use of reason. Kant argues that our understanding of space and time as necessary and universal principles falls into this category.

Furthermore, Kant distinguishes between phenomena and noumena. Phenomena are the appearances of objects as they are experienced by us, shaped by our senses and the forms of intuition. Noumena, on the other hand, are the things in themselves, unknowable by us due to the limitations of our cognitive faculties.

Overall, Kant's transcendental aesthetic provides a crucial framework for understanding how our perception of space and time influences our understanding of reality. It highlights the role of intuition and reason in shaping our experience of the world and emphasizes the limitations of our knowledge in accessing the true nature of things.

Husserl's Phenomenology of Time

Edmund Husserl, a prominent figure in the field of phenomenology, delved deep into exploring the nature of time and its connection to consciousness. Let us examine Husserl's unique approach to understanding time through the lens of phenomenology.

Phenomenology is a philosophical framework that aims to understand the structures of consciousness and the ways in which we experience the world around us. Husserl believed that by focusing on the subjective experience of time, we can gain insights into the fundamental nature of reality itself.

In his investigations, Husserl emphasized the importance of bracketing or setting aside preconceived notions and biases when studying consciousness. He proposed the concept of phenomenological reduction, which involves suspending judgments and assumptions to explore the pure essence of the phenomena being studied.

According to Husserl, we experience time in a unique and subjective manner. He argued that time cannot be reduced to a mere physical entity or a mathematical construct, but rather, it is intimately tied to our consciousness. Time, for Husserl, is not just a measurement of duration but a lived experience.

Time is a fundamental aspect of our existence, influencing our thoughts, actions, and perceptions. In this section, we will delve deeper into the subjective nature of time and its intricate connection to conscious experience.

Husserl's phenomenological approach sheds light on the notion that time is not an objective entity but a subjective phenomenon. He believed that time is experienced through our consciousness, influencing how we perceive and understand the world.

One key element of Husserl's analysis is the concept of the now. The now is the present moment, the fleeting instant in which our consciousness is perpetually situated. Husserl argues that our experience of time is rooted in this ongoing stream of nows, where past moments become memories and future moments become anticipations.

Furthermore, Husserl explored the concept of intentionality in relation to time. Intentionality refers to the directedness of consciousness towards objects or experiences. In the realm of time, intentionality allows us to project ourselves into the future, recollect past experiences, and perceive the passage of time.

By emphasizing the subjective nature of time and its connection to conscious experience, Husserl invites us to reflect on the profound influence time has on our perception of reality. Through phenomenology, he encourages us to explore the intricate interplay between subjective experiences of time and the fundamental nature of existence.

Husserl's Phenomenology of Time

Husserl's phenomenology of time offers a unique perspective on the nature of temporal experience. In this section, we will delve deeper into Husserl's insights and theories surrounding time within the context of phenomenology.

One key aspect of Husserl's phenomenology of time is the concept of protention and retention. Protention refers to our anticipation of future events, while retention refers to our recollection of past events. These temporal modes are considered essential components of our subjective experience of time.

According to Husserl, our conscious awareness of time is not limited to the present moment. Through protention, we actively project ourselves into the future, allowing us to anticipate upcoming events and plan accordingly. Similarly, through retention, we retain and recall past experiences, shaping our understanding of the present moment.

Husserl also emphasizes the role of subjective time-consciousness in shaping our perception of the world. Our consciousness of time allows us to recognize the temporal order of events and to distinguish between past, present, and future. Time-consciousness acts as a foundation for our overall experience of reality.

By exploring the complex relationship between temporal experience and consciousness, Husserl's phenomenology provides valuable insights into the nature of time. His theories invite us to reflect on the subjective dimensions of time and its significance in shaping our lived experiences.

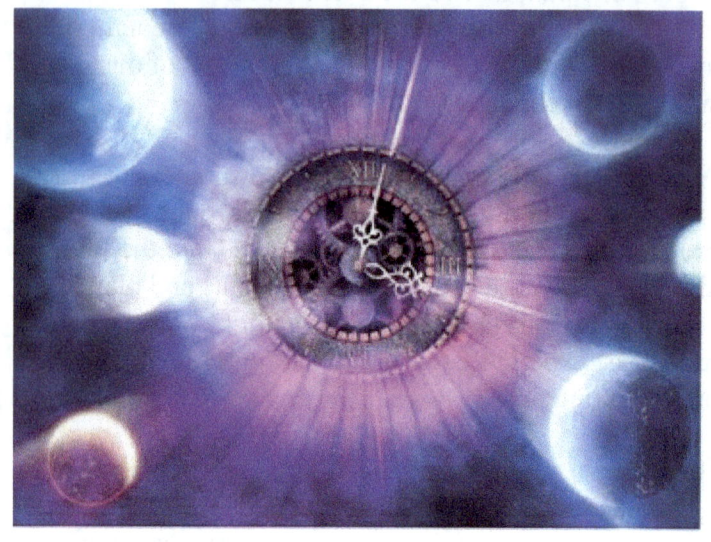

All consciousness is consciousness of something.

— Edmund Husserl

Chapter 13: Unification of Space, Time, and Consciousness

Consciousness and Space-Time

Throughout human history, there has been an ongoing fascination with the nature of consciousness and the fabric of space-time. Exploring the relationship between these two enigmatic concepts has been a subject of great interest for philosophers, scientists, and metaphysicists alike. We will now examine the intriguing connection between consciousness and space-time, shedding light on how they may intertwine and shape our understanding of the universe.

To comprehend the association between consciousness and space-time, we must first establish a basic understanding of both concepts. Space-time refers to the four-dimensional framework in which all physical events occur. It blends the three dimensions of space with the dimension of time into a single interwoven continuum. On the other hand, consciousness refers to our subjective awareness, thoughts, and experiences that make up our individual reality.

One fascinating theory that attempts to bridge the gap between consciousness and space-time is the idea that consciousness may play a fundamental role in shaping the fabric of space-time itself. The theory of Biocentrism, proposed by Robert Lanza, is a radical and controversial idea that challenges traditional understandings of the universe. Unlike most scientific theories that place physics at the foundation of the universe, Biocentrism argues that consciousness and life are fundamental, and the universe itself is a product of these.

According to this viewpoint, consciousness is not merely a byproduct of physical processes but is intricately intertwined with the underlying structure of reality. This theory posits that consciousness may influence the perception of space and time, with our conscious experiences and observations actively shaping the very nature of the universe.

Furthermore, some philosophers and physicists propose that the nature of consciousness may hold clues to understanding the fundamental nature of space and time. The subjective nature of conscious experience presents a unique challenge to our understanding of reality. How do we reconcile the subjective and often ambiguous nature of our conscious experiences with the objective and measurable world described by physics? This question has sparked debates about the nature of reality and the role of consciousness in shaping our perception of it.

In recent years, scientific research has begun to shed light on the intricate relationship between consciousness and space-time. Studies in neuroscience, psychology, and physics have provided valuable insights into how our conscious experiences are influenced by the physical world around us. From the way our brains process sensory information to the perception of time during altered states of consciousness, researchers are uncovering the complex interplay between our subjective experience and the objective reality we inhabit.

Overall, the relationship between consciousness and space-time is a deeply intriguing and multifaceted topic that continues to captivate the minds of researchers and thinkers. By exploring this connection, we gain a deeper understanding of the fundamental nature of reality and the role that our subjective experiences play in shaping our understanding of the universe. In the following chapters, we will continue our exploration, examining other aspects of consciousness and its implications for our perception of reality.

The Spiritual Dimensions of Time

In different belief systems, time holds significant spiritual and philosophical implications. It is viewed as a fundamental aspect of the human experience and a reflection of deeper truths about existence. Let us explore how different belief systems perceive the concept of time.

In many spiritual traditions, time is seen as more than just a linear progression from past to present to future. It is often regarded as a sacred and mysterious force that connects the physical and metaphysical realms. Time is seen as a vessel through which divine wisdom and understanding can be accessed.

Eastern philosophical traditions, such as Hinduism and Buddhism, the concept of time is closely tied to the cyclical nature of existence. These belief systems recognize the interconnectedness of all beings and emphasize the eternal cycle of birth, death, and rebirth. Time, in this context, is seen as an illusion that humans must transcend in order to achieve enlightenment.

In contrast, monotheistic religions like Christianity, Islam, and Judaism view time as a linear progression with a definite beginning and end. The idea of an apocalyptic event or a final judgment day marks the culmination of this linear timeline. Time is seen as a limited resource, meant to be utilized wisely in the pursuit of spiritual growth and the fulfillment of divine purpose.

Indigenous belief systems also offer unique perspectives on the spiritual dimensions of time. Many indigenous cultures perceive time as a sacred circle, where past, present, and future coexist. They believe that the actions of ancestors continue to influence the present and that future generations will inherit the consequences of our current actions. Time is regarded as a powerful force that connects individuals to their ancestors and descendants, reminding them of their responsibilities and the importance of living in harmony with nature.

Sikhism, a monotheistic religion founded in the 15th century in the Punjab region of India, has unique perspectives on concepts such as space, time, and consciousness. These ideas are deeply rooted in the teachings of the Sikh Gurus and the holy scripture, the Guru Granth Sahib.

In Sikhism, space and time are seen as creations of God, with God existing beyond these constructs as the eternal, omnipresent being. Consciousness is viewed as a divine attribute present within each individual, with the goal being to realize and unite with the Supreme Consciousness. Sikh scripture often speaks of countless worlds and universes, suggesting a view of a vast, infinite cosmos. This aligns with the modern scientific view of a possibly infinite universe. Through meditation, ethical living, and devotion, Sikhs strive to transcend the illusions of the material world and achieve spiritual enlightenment.

The Dogon people of Mali, West South Africa have a rich body of myths explaining the cosmos, humanity's origin, and their place in the universe. These stories are passed down through generations through oral traditions, music, and art. Some early claims suggested the Dogon possessed advanced astronomical knowledge about Sirius, a binary star system. This has been heavily debated, with some suggesting misinterpretations or outside influences.

The Dogon people offer a unique glimpse into a culture deeply connected to its environment, ancestors, and a rich spiritual belief system. While some Dogon villages retain their traditional way of life, others are experiencing modernization and changes in religious practices.

Overall, exploring the spiritual dimensions of time reveals its deep significance in various belief systems. It serves as a pathway to divine knowledge, a means of achieving enlightenment, and a reminder of our interconnectedness with the past and future. This understanding invites us to reflect on our own relationship with time and how it can shape our spiritual journey.

Yoga and Meditation

By understanding the deeper aspects of these practices, we can gain a profound insight into the interconnectedness of all things.

Yoga and meditation have been practiced for centuries and have become increasingly popular in today's fast-paced world. These practices offer a way to bring balance and harmony to our lives, fostering a greater understanding of ourselves and the world around us.

Yoga, in its essence, is about the union of mind, body, and spirit. It involves physical postures, breath control, and meditation techniques that help to cultivate a sense of deep awareness and inner peace. By engaging in yoga, we learn to connect with our bodies and become more attuned to the present moment.

Meditation, on the other hand, is a practice of focusing one's mind and achieving a state of deep relaxation and heightened awareness. Through various techniques such as mindfulness, concentration, and visualization, meditation allows us to transcend the limitations of time and space and explore the realms of consciousness.

When we practice yoga and meditation, we begin to realize that space and time are not fixed concepts but rather fluid and interdependent. We start to recognize that our experience of space and time is influenced by our consciousness and perception. As we cultivate a deeper awareness through these practices, we become more attuned to the interconnectedness of all things.

Yoga and meditation teach us to observe and embrace the present moment without judgment or attachment. By quieting the mind and letting go of distractions, we can tap into a state of pure awareness where we experience a sense of unity with everything around us. This shift in consciousness allows us to recognize that we are not separate from the world but an integral part of it.

Through the practices of yoga and meditation, we discover that space and time are not obstacles but rather gateways to deeper understanding and connection. As we explore the dimensions of consciousness, we begin to perceive the interplay between space, time, and metaphysics. This understanding opens up new realms of possibility and offers a profound insight into the nature of reality.

The practices of yoga and meditation offer a unique lens through which we can explore the interconnections of space, time, and consciousness. By engaging in these practices, we can cultivate a deeper awareness of our place in the world and foster a sense of unity with that universe.

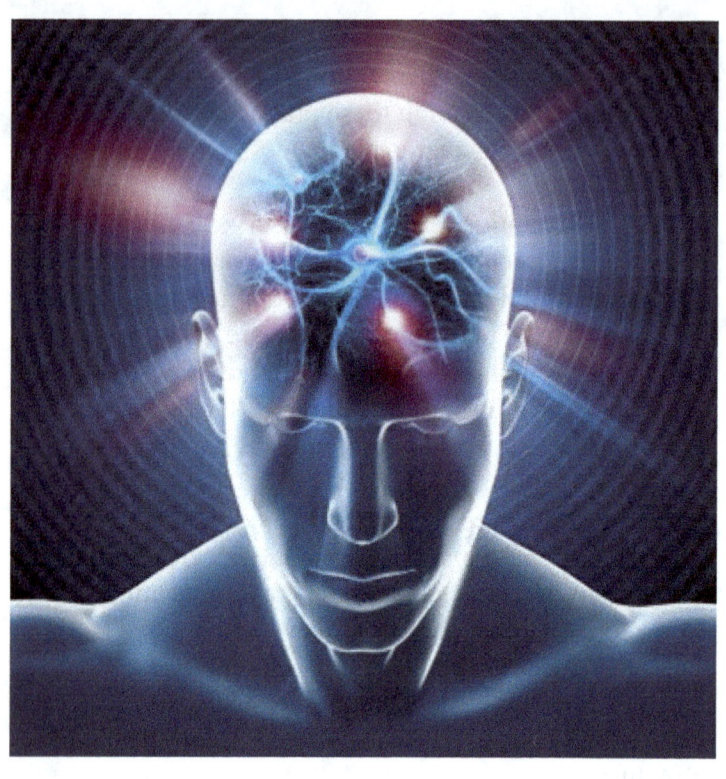

"Time is an illusion. Time only exists when we think
about the past and the future. Time doesn't exist in
the present here and now."

— Marina Abramovic

About the Author

Omar Lopez is an author and philosopher whose work delves into the profound intersections of space, time, and consciousness. Currently residing in the serene Pocono Mountains, Omar finds inspiration in the natural beauty surrounding him. His days and nights are dedicated to exploring and writing about the mysteries of the universe and the human mind. With a passion for unraveling complex ideas and making them accessible, Omar's writing invites readers to embark on a journey of discovery and reflection.

GLOSSARY OF TERMS

Absolute Time: The concept of a universal, unchanging time that progresses at a constant rate, independent of any external influences or observers.

Anthropic Principle: The idea that the universe's laws and parameters are fine-tuned to allow for the existence of life, particularly human life.

Astrophysics: The branch of astronomy concerned with the physical properties and processes of celestial objects and phenomena.

Big Bang: The prevailing cosmological model that explains the early development of the universe, positing that it began as a singularity approximately 13.8 billion years ago and has been expanding ever since.

Black Hole: A region in space where the gravitational pull is so strong that nothing, not even light, can escape from it.

Block Universe: A theory of time where past, present, and future events coexist equally in a four-dimensional space-time, sometimes referred to as the "eternalism" theory.

Brain Waves: Electrical impulses in the brain that can be measured and are associated with different states of consciousness.

Causality: The relationship between cause and effect, fundamental in understanding the sequence and interaction of events in time and space.

Chronology: The science of arranging events in their order of occurrence in time.

Cognitive Science: The interdisciplinary study of the mind and its processes, including aspects of psychology, artificial intelligence, philosophy, neuroscience, and linguistics.

Consciousness: The state of being aware of and able to think about one's own existence, thoughts, and surroundings.

Cosmic Microwave Background Radiation (CMB): The thermal radiation left over from the time of recombination in Big Bang cosmology, providing a snapshot of the early universe.

Cosmic String: A hypothetical one-dimensional defect in space-time thought to have formed during phase transitions in the early universe.

Cosmology: The scientific study of the origin, evolution, and eventual fate of the universe.

Dark Energy: A mysterious form of energy that is hypothesized to permeate all of space and is responsible for the accelerated expansion of the universe.

Dark Matter: A type of matter that does not emit, absorb, or reflect light, making it invisible, but whose presence can be inferred from its gravitational effects on visible matter.

Dualism: The philosophical concept that mind and body are distinct and separable entities.

Electromagnetic Spectrum: The range of all types of electromagnetic radiation, from gamma rays to radio waves.

Entropy: A measure of the amount of disorder or randomness in a system, often associated with the second law of thermodynamics.

Epiphenomenalism: The theory that mental phenomena are caused by physical processes in the brain but do not themselves cause any physical events.

Event Horizon: The boundary surrounding a black hole beyond which nothing can escape its gravitational pull.

General Relativity: Albert Einstein's theory of gravitation, which describes gravity as a curvature of space-time caused by mass and energy.

Gravitational Lensing: The bending of light from a distant source around a massive object between the source and the observer.

Gravitational Waves: Ripples in space-time caused by some of the most violent and energetic processes in the universe, such as colliding black holes.

Hawking Radiation: Theoretical radiation predicted by Stephen Hawking, which is emitted by black holes due to quantum effects near the event horizon.

Heisenberg Uncertainty Principle: A fundamental principle of quantum mechanics stating that it is impossible to simultaneously know the exact position and momentum of a particle.

Holographic Principle: A theory suggesting that all of the information contained within a volume of space can be represented as a hologram—a two-dimensional surface that can encode the three-dimensional information.

Interstellar Medium: The matter and radiation that exist in the space between the star systems in a galaxy.

Light Cone: A diagram depicting the possible locations and paths of light signals emanating from a given event in space-time.

Light Year: The distance that light travels in one year, approximately 9.46 trillion kilometers (5.88 trillion miles).

Lorentz Transformation: The mathematical relationship that describes how measurements of space and time by two observers are related to each other in special relativity.

Many-Worlds Interpretation: An interpretation of quantum mechanics that posits the existence of many worlds, each representing different outcomes of quantum measurements.

Multiverse: The hypothetical set of multiple possible universes, including our own, that together comprise everything that exists.

Neurons: Nerve cells in the brain and nervous system that transmit information through electrical and chemical signals.

Nonlocality: A property of quantum mechanics where particles can be instantaneously correlated with each other regardless of the distance separating them.

Observable Universe: The region of the universe that can be observed from Earth or its space-based instruments, limited by the speed of light.

Parallel Universes: Hypothetical self-contained universes that exist alongside our own and may operate under different physical laws.

Perception: The process of recognizing, organizing, and interpreting sensory information.

Phenomenology: The philosophical study of the structures of experience and consciousness.

Photoelectric Effect: The emission of electrons or other free carriers when light shines on a material, a phenomenon explained by quantum mechanics.

Planck Time: The time it takes for light to travel one Planck length, considered the smallest measurable unit of time.

Quantum Decoherence: The process by which a quantum system loses its quantum behavior and transitions to classical behavior due to interaction with its environment.

Quantum Entanglement: A physical phenomenon occurring when pairs or groups of particles interact in ways such that the quantum state of each particle cannot be described independently of the others.

Quantum Field Theory: The theoretical framework for constructing quantum mechanical models of subatomic particles in particle physics and quantum fields.

Quantum Mechanics: The branch of physics that deals with the behavior of particles on the atomic and subatomic scale.

Redshift: The phenomenon where light from an object is increased in wavelength, or shifted to the red end of the spectrum, often used to indicate that an object is moving away from the observer.

Relativity: The dependence of various physical phenomena on the relative motion of the observer and the observed objects, encompassing both the special and general theories of relativity.

Singularity: A point in space-time where gravitational forces cause matter to have an infinite density and zero volume, often associated with the centers of black holes.

Space-Time Continuum: The four-dimensional continuum in which all events take place and all things exist, combining the three dimensions of space and one dimension of time.

Special Relativity: Albert Einstein's theory that describes the physics of moving bodies and incorporates the principle that the laws of physics are the same for all non-accelerating observers.

String Theory: A theoretical framework in which particles are described not as points but as one-dimensional strings, whose vibrations determine the particles' properties.

Subjectivity: The quality of being based on or influenced by personal feelings, tastes, or opinions.

Superposition Principle: The principle in quantum mechanics that a physical system exists simultaneously in all its possible states until it is measured.

Synaptic Plasticity: The ability of synapses (the connections between neurons) to strengthen or weaken over time in response to increases or decreases in their activity.

Tachyons: Hypothetical particles that travel faster than light.

Teleportation: The theoretical transfer of matter or energy from one point to another without traversing the physical space between them.

Theory of Everything (TOE): A hypothetical single, all-encompassing, coherent theoretical framework of physics that fully explains and links together all physical aspects of the universe.

Time Dilation: A difference in the elapsed time measured by two observers, due to a relative difference in velocity or the presence of a gravitational field.

Time Travel: The concept of moving between different points in time, akin to moving between different points in space.

Uncertainty Principle: The principle that it is impossible to simultaneously know both the exact position and the exact momentum of a particle.

Unified Field Theory: A type of field theory that allows all of the fundamental forces and particles to be written in terms of a single theoretical framework.

Wave-Particle Duality: The principle in quantum mechanics that every particle or quantum entity may be described as either a particle or a wave.

Wheeler-DeWitt Equation: A field equation that combines quantum mechanics and general relativity, often used in the study of quantum gravity.

White Hole: A hypothetical region of space-time which cannot be entered from the outside, although matter and light can escape from it.

Wormhole: A hypothetical tunnel-like structure connecting two separate points in space-time, potentially allowing travel between them faster than light could in normal space-time.

Zeitgeber: An environmental cue, such as light or temperature, that helps to regulate the biological clock in organisms.